#3 THE HAUNTED HOUSE

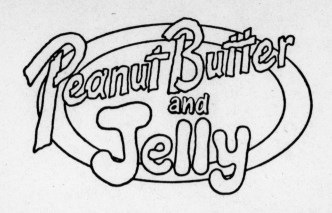

#3 THE HAUNTED HOUSE

Dorothy Haas

Illustrated by Jeffrey Lindberg

A
LITTLE APPLE
PAPERBACK

SCHOLASTIC INC.
New York Toronto London Auckland Sydney

ISBN 0-590-41508-5

12 11 10 9 8 7 6 5 4 3 2 1   8 9/8 0 1 2 3/9

Printed in the U.S.A.   28

First Scholastic printing, November 1988

For Elizabeth and Jim,
Andrea and Joey

CHAPTER
1

"Frogs' noses." Peanut's eyes danced as she tossed a stick for Nibbsie to bring back. "Delicious," she added, smacking her lips.

"Cobwebs with creepy-crawlies on them that stick in your hair." Jilly shuddered even while she laughed. "Ick!"

"Eyeball salad," said Peanut. "And maybe some mashed brains."

"A dead man's hand that comes at you out of the dark," said Jilly.

"I know how to make the best food!" said Peanut.

1

"We've got a perfect place for a haunted house," said Jilly. "There's this old fruit cellar in our basement. It's just right."

"But will your mom let you?" asked Peanut.

"Don't know," said Jilly. "But I think so. I mean, she was awful sorry when I had strep throat and couldn't have my birthday party."

"This will be a just-for-fun party," said Peanut. "Ask her."

"As soon as I get home," Jilly promised.

Nibbsie came running, with the stick in his mouth. But when he got to Peanut, he wouldn't give it up. He hung on, growling fiercely.

"Silly," she said, trying to take it. "Either you play tug-of-war or you play run-get-the-stick. You can't go get it if you don't let me have it."

Almost as though he understood what she was saying, Nibbsie let go.

Peanut tossed the stick, careful not to send it anywhere near the kids playing touch football near the fountain or Jennifer Patimkin and her friends playing with a big sheepdog near an ancient apple tree.

Polly — better known as Peanut — Butterman and Jillian Matthews were in Lighthouse Park after school. Having a haunted house was Jilly's idea. Her father had told her about doing that when he was a boy and it was, she thought, the most fun thing she had ever heard of.

"We'll keep the fruit cellar really dark," she said. "Kids coming to the party will have to come in through the outside door and — "

Peanut interrupted. "What's a fruit cellar?"

Jilly had long ago asked that very question. "In the olden days, before there were refrigerators and freezers, people kept food in their basements because they were cool. Fruit cellars were where they stored apples and pears and things until they ate them."

"Oh," said Peanut, having another tug-of-war with Nibbsie. "Did they have vegetable cellars, too?"

Jilly didn't know about that. "But listen," she went on, getting back to the haunted house. "We've got to have an old trunk. A skeleton can jump out of it."

3

"We'll need a witch, too," said Peanut, tossing the stick. "One with glowing red eyes."

"Who has red eyes?" asked Erin, joining them.

Peanut and Jilly exchanged looks. They didn't dare let Erin in on their plans. If Erin heard, there wouldn't be any surprises left for anybody.

Jilly acted supercool. "Oh, nothing."

"We were just talking about these guys," said Peanut, leaning on the word *guys*, which sounded like *eyes*.

"I don't believe you!" Erin looked suspiciously from Peanut to Jilly and back again. "You were talking about a secret. I can tell."

"Nibbsie!" Peanut yelled, looking past Erin. "Don't!" She pushed Erin aside and raced toward the twisted old apple tree.

Jilly turned to look and ran after her.

The sheepdog had Nibbsie's stick. It was lumbering around in circles, the stick held high in its mouth. Nibbsie was on the attack, yipping wildly. The dogs looked like floor mops — the one perfectly enormous, the other

4

dollhouse-size. But there was no mistaking the fierceness of Nibbsie's bark. He was ready to take apart this stick thief.

Peanut caught him as he leaped. "No, boy! Cool it!"

Nibbsie wriggled in her arms, barking shrilly.

Peanut looked at Jennifer Patimkin over Nibbsie's head. "Please make your dog give back Nibbsie's stick."

Jennifer threw her arms around the sheepdog's neck. "Are you all right, Baby?" she cooed.

"Baby!" exclaimed Peanut. "You call that — that — big lummox 'Baby'?"

Jennifer didn't answer. She went right on talking to Baby. "Did the awful little mutt hurt you, Baby?"

"Mutt!" Peanut was outraged. "Nibbsie's not a mutt. And he'd be insulted if I called him 'Baby'! If your dog's a baby, Nibbsie should be called a hero for taking on someone bigger than he is. And he wants his stick," she added firmly.

"It's just an old stick," Jennifer said in an

I'm-better-than-you voice. "Sticks belong to anybody who finds them."

"Not that one," Peanut said evenly, wondering if she was going to have to take the stick away from Baby. "Nibbsie was playing with it. It's his stick. I can tell by the big lump at the end of it."

At that moment Baby opened her mouth to lick Jennifer's face. The stick fell to the ground and Peanut snatched it. "Baby!" she muttered, stamping away.

Jilly followed her. "That Jennifer," she said. "She always says stuff to make a person not like her."

Peanut rubbed the stick on the grass to clean off Baby's spit and tossed it again. Nibbsie brought it back. But somehow the fun had gone out of the game.

"Come on," she said, "let's go home."

"Maybe my mom's home by now," said Jilly. "She had a parents' meeting after school, but that must be over by now."

"Don't forget to ask her," said Peanut, her

7

good nature returning. "And call me as soon as you find out."

"See? You have got a secret," said Erin, running after them. "It's something about red eyes. You're mean not to tell me."

"You'll find out soon," said Jilly, taking pity on her. "If we get to do what we think we're going to do."

Erin let out a disgusted "Huh!" as she turned toward home.

The telephone rang at the Buttermans' house shortly after dinner that evening. Peanut made a dash for it and picked it up an instant before her sister Maggie could. "The Butterman residence," she panted in her most proper-sounding voice. "Polly speaking."

She listened, then "It's for me," she whispered to Maggie, who was hanging around hoping the call was for her.

A smile spread across Peanut's face as she listened to Jilly. "We can?" she squealed. "Everything? . . . Everyone? . . . We can make the invitations tomorrow. . . . Listen — get here early. We can talk about it on the way to school. And . . . and . . . tell your mom she's the best mom in the whole world," she added before she hung up.

"She is?" asked Mrs. Butterman, who was passing through the hall. "Really?"

Peanut hugged her. "Oh, you know what I mean. Listen — Jilly's having a party because she was sick on her birthday and couldn't have one then. We're going to have a haunted house. Can I make eyeball salad? And mashed brains? I don't think she knows how to do that."

Mrs. Butterman laughed. "I'm almost sorry that you do. Your talents blow me over. But yes, I imagine that will be all right." Then she looked thoughtful. "Jilly's having an un-birthday," she said with a look that meant Peanut was supposed to catch on to something.

"Huh?" Peanut was puzzled.

"Alice?" said Mrs. Butterman. *"Through the Looking Glass?"*

They had read that book just a few months ago.

Wheels turned in Peanut's head. A light

dawned. "Humpty Dumpty," she said. "His tie. The White King and Queen gave it to him."

"For an un-birthday present," said her mother.

"You can only get birthday presents one day a year," said Peanut. "But Humpty said you can get un-birthday presents on three hundred sixty-four days."

She had an idea. A wonderful idea.

CHAPTER
2

Emmy and Erin were waiting the next morning. "Erin says you've got a secret," Emmy called as Peanut and Jilly neared the corner. "Something about somebody with red eyes."

Peanut and Jilly glanced at each other. Isn't it good we didn't tell Erin anything? their eyes seemed to say.

"Someone with red eyes?" Peanut asked innocently. She turned to Jilly. "Were we talking about anybody with red eyes?"

Jilly put on a thoughtful look. "Wasn't it some*thing* with red eyes?"

"Oh, you!" Erin exploded. "You know you were talking about a secret. And you know I sort of heard you. And you know you even said if you got to do it, I'd find out about it."

"You didn't tell me that part, Erin O'Malley," said Emmy. "About getting to do it. And I'm your very best friend."

Erin looked downcast. "I forgot. But you know you said that," she added, shaking her finger under Jilly's nose.

"So, are you getting to do the whatever it is you're going to do?" Emmy demanded.

"Red . . . eyes . . . " Jilly said slowly, looking up at the trees. "Werewolves have red eyes, don't they, Peanut?"

"Mean little red eyes," said Peanut. "White rabbits, too, only their eyes aren't mean."

"Now you're teasing," said Erin.

Emmy wouldn't let it go. "So, if you don't know yet about doing the whatever, when will you find out?"

Jilly remembered something. It was too good not to say! "My Uncle Dave always takes the red-eye special when he comes from California. That's a special plane — a red-eye plane."

"Just you see how many secrets I tell you ever again!" said Emmy. But she didn't look really mad — only as though curiosity were killing her.

Peanut and Jilly laughed.

"I'm going to follow you and listen and find out," said Emmy. "You won't be able to stop me." She and Erin dropped a few steps behind Peanut and Jilly, walking silently, watching, listening. Emmy had the go-get-'em look of a detective on a hot trail.

Before the morning was over, everybody knew that a big secret was afoot.

"I heard you've got red eyes today, Peanut," said Elena, looking at her closely as she returned to her desk from the book corner.

Peanut opened her eyes wide. They definitely were not red. She just laughed.

"Have I ever told you what gorgeous red eyes you've got?" asked Elvis as he strolled past Jilly's desk.

Jilly fluttered her eyelashes at him, and Elvis turned red and didn't say another word. He didn't even giggle.

"Is what you're going to do awful, or less than awful, or fun, or none of the above?" asked Courtney when she passed out the math papers for Miss Kraft.

"How long are we going to have to wait?" asked Nate, looking up at the clock. "I mean, are you going to tell us today, or next week, or next month?"

"Dumb girls' secret," said Ollie as they lined up to go to the lunchroom. "Us guys don't care about a dumb old girls' secret." But he kept a close eye on Peanut and Jilly.

Actually, Jilly and Peanut were having a hard time keeping the secret. It was so much fun, they were dying to tell.

"Maybe," said Jilly as she led the way to a place in one corner of the lunchroom where they could be alone, "maybe we better not wait till after school to make the invitations. Should we make them during free study?"

14

She had to say that in three whispered parts
as Emmy and then Erin came close and tried
to hear what they were talking about.

"Making an invitation for each person sure
will be lots of work," said Peanut. She had to
stop talking while Elena walked slowly past
them. Then she asked, "Why don't we make a
big one — "

"A big one with red eyes?" asked Elvis as he strolled past with his tray.

Peanut rolled her eyes and waited until he was out of earshot. " — and ask Miss Kraft to put it on the bulletin board when school lets out?" she finished.

That seemed like a good idea. So then they whispered about what to put on the invitation. It was very hard to talk, with everybody walking past them and trying to hear.

"I can make the picture," said Jilly. "A big one of a haunted house."

"I'll do the writing part," said Peanut. "We can fasten it to the picture."

"Make it so it will fit on the door," said Jilly. "I'll show you how big."

So, during free study, Jilly got out her felt-tip pens and drew a rickety-looking house with sagging shutters and a ghost looking out of one of the windows. One by one people found reasons to walk past her, peeking at what she was doing. Nobody paid any attention to Peanut, who was, after all, just writing something.

She printed carefully:

You are invited to an un-birthday party
at the haunted house. Be ready to be
Scared. Be ready to Shiver. Be ready to
scream a lot. Only brave people welcome.

She sat back and read what she had written.
It looked really good. *Haunted house* and *scared*
and *shiver* and *scream* were made with squiggly
letters. Suddenly she had a really great idea.
She went to Jilly and whispered close to her
ear.

Jilly listened, her face lighting up. "That'll
make things even more fun," she whispered
back.

Peanut returned to her desk and wrote:

You have to wear a costume and a mask
and you can't take off the mask until
somebody wins a prize for the best
costume.

Under that she wrote: *A week from today,
Friday*, 6 P.M. to 8:30 P.M., and signed Jilly's
name.

There! The words were going to look really neat on the door of the house Jilly had drawn.

Together, Peanut and Jilly went to ask Miss Kraft if she would put the invitation on the bulletin board.

She read it thoughtfully. "So this is what's had everyone on pins and needles today." She sighed. "I can't stand another day like this one. Okay, I'll put up the invitation just before the last bell."

She was as good as her word, and everybody watched while she thumbtacked the haunted house to the board.

When the final bell jangled, there was a rush to the bulletin board.

"Hey, neat," said David, grinning.

"Never shivered or screamed in my whole life," said Ollie, trying to look bored.

"But," asked Erin, "where's the part about red eyes?"

"You'll see," said Jilly.

Erin shivered. And she was only *thinking* about the haunted house.

CHAPTER
3

■■■■■■■■■■■
■ ■ ■ ■ ■ ■

'Talking about making a haunted house . . . and thinking about making a haunted house . . . were a whole lot easier than actually making a haunted house. Peanut and Jilly soon found that out.

First they explored the fruit cellar. It was just one small room with shelves on two sides and a single light bulb in the ceiling. A door on one wall opened out into the backyard. Another door led from the fruit cellar into the basement.

The basement had been fixed up a long time

ago as a kind of rough-and-ready room for Jilly and her brothers. They called it the "wreck" room. Jilly roller-skated there when the sidewalks outdoors were wet or covered with snow. Jackie rode his tricycle there. And there was a basketball hoop for Jerry, even though the ceiling was low. The furniture had come from other parts of the house. It was old, so it didn't matter if anybody put their feet on it or jumped on it or anything.

"Mom says everybody will have to stay down here," Jilly explained. "But that's okay. There's lots of room for games, and it won't matter if somebody spills something."

They went back into the fruit cellar and sat on a couple of boxes.

"It's kind of grim in here," said Peanut, looking around at the old brick walls. She grinned. "That's perfect. Grim, I mean."

"It's just this one room, though," said Jilly. "We've got to have sort of" — she spoke slowly, thinking — "well, corners for scary things, a kind of hallway to walk through. How can we make a hallway?"

"Boxes from the Jewel?" asked Peanut, looking as though she didn't think that was the answer at all. "You know — open them up flat to make walls."

"We've got an old carpet up in the back hall," Jilly said thoughtfully. "We could hang it over a clothesline for a wall — if we had a clothesline."

"Old curtains — that's what we can use!" Peanut was excited. "I heard my mom tell my grandma that the curtains from our old place don't fit the windows in the new house."

"We can use sheets, too," said Jilly. "I bet we've got some old ones. We can hang them over clotheslines. I'll ask my dad to put up some clotheslines."

"What else do we need?" asked Peanut.

"A skeleton." That was one thing Jilly was certain about.

"And the trunk for it to jump out of at people," said Peanut.

"We better have a witch," said Jilly. "One with glowing red eyes, or everybody will be disappointed."

21

"I wish we could fix a werewolf," said Peanut. "Do you know what a werewolf looks like? Hey! Maybe we can do something with Bumpy or Bonkers. Cats' eyes glow in the dark. Spooooo-keeee!"

"You can't be mean to Bonkers." Peanut and Jilly looked up. It was Jackie, sitting on his tricycle, licking a Popsicle. "She doesn't like to be dressed up."

"Don't worry, Jack-O," said Jilly. "We won't hurt old Bonkers. You can't dress up cats," she added for Peanut's information. "Whoever writes those storybooks about cats in doll clothes didn't ever have a cat."

"I like to dress up, though," said Jackie between slurps of his Popsicle. "Daddy said he's going to paint my face and I'll be a black cat. Everyone at the party is going to be very surprised."

A five-year-old at a big kids' party? The kids would be surprised for sure! Oh, pickle juice!

"Listen, Jack-O," said Jilly, "you won't want to come to this party. We'll just be doing dull big-kid stuff."

23

"Yes, I do," said Jackie, wiping his red chin with the back of his hand. "I'm practically a big kid. Mrs. Potter said so today when I ate all my soup and nine crackers besides."

Jilly sighed. She was going to have to figure out what to do about Jackie. Along with everything else. Like how to make a dead man's hand touch people in the dark. And how to make the skeleton pop out of the trunk. If she could find a skeleton and a trunk. There had to be a prize for the best costume, too, and food to eat. Real food — not just eyeball salad and frogs' noses.

Word swept through Louisa May Alcott. Jilly Matthews was going to have a haunted house party. What a tremendous idea!

But then a second wave of words followed the first. Jilly's house wasn't big enough for all the children at school. Only those in Miss Kraft's class were invited to the party.

"See if I care," sniffed Jennifer Patimkin, who was in Mr. Moore's class. "Who ever heard of an un-birthday party?"

"I wouldn't be caught dead in a haunted house," said her friend Cheryl.

"It's all just too childish," Dawn added in a bored voice.

Jennifer and Cheryl and Dawn wore purple nail polish after that and practiced dance steps and tried to act too grown-up for a haunted house party.

Elvis and Ollie and Emmy and Erin didn't seem to think haunted house parties were babyish, though. They prowled around the Matthewses' yard and tried to peek in the basement windows.

Peanut and Jilly could hear them laughing and talking outside. Jilly brought one of the pillows from the wreck room and stuffed it against the window in the fruit cellar, and then nobody on the outside could see what was happening on the inside.

And things began to happen.

Mr. Matthews did string clotheslines around the fruit cellar. He draped Butterman curtains and Matthews sheets over them to make a winding sort of hallway with nooks and crannies. And he covered the light bulb with a shade that looked like a skull. The haunted house became dark and spooky.

Jilly found a skeleton at K mart, left over from Halloween, and on sale, too! It was made of cardboard and came in pieces — arm bones and leg bones and a spine and a skull. She joined the pieces with clips so that the skeleton's arm bones and leg bones were loose and jiggly.

Peanut's grandpa had an old trunk, and he most obligingly brought it to the Matthewses' and put it in the haunted house. But how to make the skeleton jump up out of the trunk?

Peanut's sister Ceci turned out to be very helpful. She was learning to make her own clothes and knew interesting things about elastic. A piece of elastic could be fastened to the skeleton's head and hooked inside the trunk. When someone unhooked it, the skeleton would pop up and jiggle.

Ceci knew a lot about yarn and cutting up old panty hose for cobwebs, too. And she had some small bits of Velcro to fasten to the cobwebs, to catch in people's hair.

With each new thing they added to the haunted house, Jilly and Peanut became more excited. They figured out what to do with the dead man's hand and how to make a bat zing through the air. One of the best things was the hairy tunnel, lined with an old fur coat. Everybody would have to crawl through it. And it took care of Jackie, too.

Mrs. Matthews had said that Jackie was welcome at any party at the Matthews house. Jackie was going to sit on the floor outside the hairy tunnel, where nobody could see him, and poke his arms through the tunnel and pat people's faces when they crawled through it.

The kids at school stopped prowling around the Matthewses' yard. But then there was a lot of whispering about costumes. Miss Kraft sighed and said she was losing her patience and was going to make everybody write special reports if they didn't settle down and learn something, for heaven's sake.

They settled down. Or they tried to.

But then Peanut told Emmy and Erin about un-birthday presents, and they told everybody else. There was more whispering — only never in front of Jilly — about what un-birthday presents meant. On that day, in the afternoon, Miss Kraft put her head in her arms on her desk and looked as though she was about to have a breakdown.

Everybody felt terrible and paid attention to math for a while.

Jennifer and her friends told Erin who told Emmy who told Peanut and Jilly that Derek Benson had invited everybody in Mr. Moore's class to a party at his house on the very night of the haunted house party.

"I guess they're going to dance a lot," said Emmy. "With boys, I mean." She looked thoughtful. "If they can get the boys to dance," she added.

"I'd rather go to a haunted house party any day," Erin said loyally. "I mean, rather than dance with a boy."

Peanut and Jilly were having too much fun

with the haunted house to care what old Jennifer Patimkin did.

At last, all that was left to do was make the food. The evening before the party Jilly helped her mother bake haunted house gingerbread squares. Peanut made the eyeball salad and the frogs' noses and some bats' blood to drink. They talked about it on the phone.

"I made the frogs' noses out of pasta shells," Peanut said. "I cooked them in green water. They're really gross," she added happily.

"I tried to make the roofs and windows on the houses with blue frosting," said Jilly. "Only it looked terrible. So I added red and now everything is kind of purple."

"My mom wouldn't let me make enough frogs' noses for everybody," said Peanut. "She said nobody would really eat them and I couldn't waste good food, and so I could only make a few."

And then Mrs. Matthews told Jilly she had to hang up and go to bed or she would be too sleepy to have fun at the party the next night.

CHAPTER 4

■▼■▼■▼■▼■▼■▼■▼■▼■▼■▼■▼■

Jilly was a witch and Peanut was a ghoul. They couldn't wear masks because they had to see to lead people through the haunted house, so Mr. Matthews had painted their faces. Standing in the eerie light of the haunted house, they looked at each other with satisfaction.

"You're so ugly you're gorgeous!" Jilly giggled. "A green face really becomes you."

"That wart on your chin does a lot for you," said Peanut. "You've got so many wrinkles you look like you're ninety million years old."

"I wish I could have figured out a way to make my eyes glow in the dark," said Jilly.

"That glow-in-the-dark tape below your eyes is pretty good, though," said Peanut.

"How do I look? How do I look?" Jackie hopped up and down, a long curving cat's tail swinging around his ankles. He was wearing a black helmet with pointy ears, his nose had become a painted black cat's nose, and he had cat whiskers.

"Like one of our 'B' cats," said Jilly. "We'll call you Blackie instead of Jackie. Now remember — "

"Is this the right door?"

"Of course it is, lunkhead. We've been casing the joint all week."

The voices came from outside.

"When are they going to let us in?"

"Has anybody gone inside yet?"

"Listen — don't act scared."

"Scared! Who's gonna be scared?"

Peanut and Jilly listened, laughing.

"How will we know when everybody's out there?" asked Peanut.

31

"It won't matter," said Jilly. "We'll just take them through the haunted house until nobody's left outside."

"Let's let them come in two at a time," said Peanut. "That way they can hang on to each other when they get terrified."

"Ready, Jack-O?" asked Jilly. "Now remember, reach through the holes in the hairy tunnel and pat people when they crawl through."

Jackie disappeared into the space beside the tunnel. "It's real dark in here," he called. "I wish I had my flashlight. I couldn't find it. Maybe I'll get scared."

"No you won't," Peanut said soothingly. "You know all the tricks. And you're the one who's going to scare people — they aren't going to scare you."

"Okay?" said Jilly, her hand on the doorknob. "Countdown. Ten, nine, eight, seven, six — "

"You're counting backwards," came a muffled complaint. "I can only count ahead, not back."

" — five, four, three, two, one!"

32

With wild shrieks, Peanut and Jilly pushed the door open and leaped outside.

The cluster of ballerinas, karate fighters, hobos, and horrible beasts stepped back. A nervous titter ran through the group.

"Silly people!" Jilly spoke in a witchy whine. "Are you ready to walk into terrible danger?"

Peanut hopped around, her knuckles on the ground. "Eh-heh-heh," she laughed in a low, gurgly voice. "Awful things are going to happen here tonight."

Jilly swung her arm around, pointing her forefinger, which sported a two-inch-long fingernail. "Who will be the first?" She let the finger stop in front of two space aliens. "Come . . . with . . . me."

One of the aliens stepped forward, tugging at the other, who hung back. "It's only Jilly, Er — uh. See? It's really just Jilly."

"Do we have to be the first ones?" wailed the other space alien, shaking its head, its feeler quivering.

Two karate fighters elbowed their way forward. "We'll go. Let us go first."

"I . . . choose . . . you." Jilly stepped closer to the aliens, rubbing her hands together and laughing evilly. "Come with me."

Nervously the space aliens followed her into the haunted house.

"Hang on to the door," Jilly whispered as she passed Peanut, "so they don't all come piling in at once. I'll be back pretty soon. Then it'll be your turn."

The door closed behind them, and Jilly flicked the switch on a tape recorder hidden behind the curtains. A low moan filled the fruit cellar, and the space aliens clutched each other.

"That is the ghost who lives in my house," croaked Jilly. "Keep moving or he'll get you."

Emmy and Erin — for that's who the space aliens were — stepped forward and right into cobwebs dangling from the ceiling.

"Eeeek!" screeched Emmy, brushing at her face. "What's in here?"

"Something's on my head!" gasped Erin, pushing wildly at the Velcro bits on the cob-webs.

"Spiders," Jilly intoned. "Tarantulas." She

let the bat swing loose on its elastic cord. Cackles came from the tape recorder.

Emmy and Erin shuddered.

"You can get away from the tarantulas by following me through the hairy tunnel," said Jilly.

She went first — and found it was hard to crawl in her long skirt. Her knees kept getting caught in the cloth. She finally bunched the skirt around her middle — as small hands in furry mittens patted her face. Hastily she moved on.

"Something's touching me!" shrieked Emmy, behind her. "Get away from me — get away from me!"

A soft laugh and a meow came from the darkness.

"I'm not going in there," wailed Erin, still on the other side of the hairy tunnel. "What happens in there?"

"Aw, come on, Erin," coaxed Emmy. "You've got to come through."

"If you don't," Jilly said in her witchiest voice, "you'll just have to stay there with the tarantulas crawling all over you."

Suddenly a piercing shriek from the tape recorder split the air.

Erin dived into the hairy tunnel, gasping, "Who's touching me? Who's doing that?"

Looking frazzled, her mask askew, she emerged into the dim light, stood up, and clutched Emmy. "There's something alive in there," she chattered, pointing at the tunnel.

"You are almost safe," cackled Jilly. She stepped near the trunk. "Almost. But I warn you not to look in this old trunk."

Emmy tiptoed forward, dragging Erin after her. As they neared the trunk, Jilly reached in and unhooked the elastic holding the skeleton in place. Released, it popped into the air, bouncing, its bony arms and legs jiggling wildly.

Emmy's and Erin's screams drowned out mad laughter from the tape recorder. They backed away from the skeleton.

"You are safe at last," Jilly crooned, opening the door to the wreck room. "You can wait here for the others to come — if they don't die of fright in the haunted house."

Emmy and Erin crowded past her into the cheerfully lighted room decorated with party streamers.

"It's okay to eat the popcorn," Jilly said in her own voice. "I'll be back pretty soon."

She closed the door, hooked the skeleton in place so it could jump out of the trunk again, and crawled back through the hairy tunnel.

"I scared them a lot," said a small voice on the other side of the tunnel.

"You were great, Jack-O," said Jilly. "Now get ready. Some more kids are coming."

Only as she passed it did Jilly remember the dead man's hand — she had forgotten to touch Emmy and Erin with it.

The tape recorder was still going, and moans and ear-piercing screeches filled the haunted house.

On the other side of the door, outside, the rest of the guests listened to all that weird noise and wondered what was going on in the haunted house.

CHAPTER
5

■ ■ ■ ■ ■ ■ ■ ■ ■
 ■ ■ ■ ■ ■ ■ ■ ■

Peanut and Jilly took turns. One always waited at the door and kept everybody outside while the other led people through the shadowy maze. Highly interesting sounds kept exploding from the haunted house.

"EEEE-yiii!" The bloody-murder screech could have cut through solid steel. "Mumble-mumble . . . cold hand on . . . mumble . . . "

" . . . scared of . . . mumble . . . dead man's mumble . . . "

"Aw, it is not . . . mumble . . . touch . . . mumble . . . "

" . . . no you don't!"

Everyone waiting outside the door heard the howls and screams and shivered and wondered what was happening. The kids in the wreck room heard the noises, too. But they knew what was going on — and that made it all the more fun. "Somebody just got to the tarantulas." "I didn't feel any cold hand. Why didn't I feel a cold hand?" "Did you feel somebody touch you in the hairy tunnel? Who was that?"

They were quiet, listening.

"Yi! Something's flying around in here. A bat! A bat!"

"It's not real, Dumbo. It's gotta be a rubber one."

"Neat skeleton. Awwww, its hand came off."

"Put it back to scare the next guys."

"I'm trying. I'm trying."

When the listeners heard giggles, giggles that wouldn't stop, they knew who was coming through the haunted house. "Listen. Here comes Elvis."

Before long, the wreck room became crowded. Everyone could sort of tell who was who, even though they all kept their masks on. One of the kids was awfully small, though.

"Hi, cat," said a ballerina. "Aren't you kind of little to be at this party?"

"I scared you plenty when I tickled you in the hairy tunnel."

"Was that you? How come you're not still in there?"

"I don't want to do that anymore. It's more fun out here in the wreck room. I want some popcorn."

It took a while for everybody to make the trip through the haunted house. The last ones didn't get touched in the hairy tunnel. Sometimes Jilly or Peanut forgot to let the bat fly free on its elastic or to touch somebody with the dead man's hand. But the hand wasn't much fun anyway after it lost its deathly chill and became warm and floppy and like what it really was — a rubber glove filled with water.

The skeleton jiggled itself to pieces, and the last kids emerged into the wreck room holding different pieces of the skeleton.

Peanut and Jilly stood together at last, the

haunted house behind them, pleased and proud of their success. The wreck room was noisy with music from the record player and laughter and shouting. Some of the kids were tossing popcorn at each other, and some were eating it, stuffing it into their mouths behind their masks.

There were lots of horror masks and a great abominable snowman with huge rubber feet. There were fright wigs and crazy noses and glasses with spinning eyeballs.

"You can sort of tell who everybody is," said Peanut, looking around, "even with the masks. I mean, they're all acting just like they do every day."

"That's got to be Ollie over there doing karate with Nate," said Jilly.

"And the clown must be Courtney," said Peanut. "But who do you think the hobos are? David? Kevin? Jason?"

"You know," said Jilly, "this room is awful full. It's almost like there are more kids here than we've got in our class."

Peanut laughed. "How can you tell? I mean,

how can you count them with everybody running around like crazy?"

Jilly remembered something. "Isn't it time to eat the frogs' noses and eyeball salad?"

"The stuff is all upstairs in your fridge," said Peanut. "I put salad dressing on the noses to make them nice and slimy and my mom said I had to keep them cold until people eat them."

"Let's go get it," said Jilly, and they pounded up the stairs and burst into the kitchen. They stopped short, bumping into each other when they saw all the grown-ups there.

Peanut's mother was sitting at the table with Mrs. Matthews, drinking coffee and laughing. Her grandpa and grandma were there, too, talking to Mr. Matthews. And — hey! — so was Miss Kraft and a man.

"I thought you said Miss Kraft couldn't come," Peanut whispered.

"I did," murmured Jilly. "She said she was going someplace else."

They talked behind their hands, looking at Miss Kraft.

"Is that Mr. X with her?" asked Peanut, who had only heard about Miss Kraft's boyfriend.

"Uh-huh," muttered Jilly. "Isn't he handsome?"

Miss Kraft looked at them and smiled, and suddenly they were embarrassed. Could she tell they had been talking about her?

Jilly went to her mother. "Mom, we need the eyeball salad and other stuff now. And we need cups and spoons."

"In that cabinet," said Mrs. Matthews, pointing. "In those plastic bags." She got things out of the refrigerator and set them on the table. "Do you need help carrying these downstairs?" She answered herself. "Yes, I think you do."

"I'll help," volunteered Miss Kraft. "I want to see what everybody looks like."

The noise in the wreck room stopped abruptly when Miss Kraft and Mrs. Matthews came down the stairs. Everybody looked stiff and shy, even though they saw Miss Kraft every day.

"Oh, my," she said, walking around. "Will

45

you just look at all of you! What a schnozzola," she laughed, tweaking a very long nose. "And isn't that a face anyone would love to kiss?" she said, blowing a kiss at the abominable snowman.

They all sort of stood around until Mrs. Matthews and Miss Kraft went back upstairs. Before the kids could start jumping again, Peanut spoke in her best ghoul voice. "Our food tonight is frogs' noses."

"Ichhh!" came from the group.

"And mashed brains and eyeball salad," she added, grinning wickedly.

The chorus was even louder. "Bleah!" "Yuck!" "Gag!"

"If you don't like any of those," Jilly croaked, "there's some delicious bats' blood for you to drink."

"Aaaaargh!" said the abominable snowman, falling down dead, until he picked himself up.

"So who will be the first to taste some of my delicious food?" gurgled Peanut.

Nobody spoke. Nobody moved.

"Oh, I do believe they are scared," Jilly cooed to Peanut.

"Scaredy cats," gurgled Peanut. "The whole bunch of them."

"Listen, you knucklehead," said one of the karate fighters. "Who are you calling scared?" He strutted to the table. "I'll have a . . ." He seemed to be choosing, looking at the ghoul food, making gagging sounds. "A frog's nose."

He picked one up, chewing noisily. "Better than McDonald's," he said, smacking his lips. "Now I need some of that bats' blood to wash it down."

He sipped, holding his nose.

After that, everybody crowded around the table. Some of them even nibbled at the ghoul food, trying to figure out what it really was.

"Aw, these aren't eyeballs. They're just peeled grapes."

"These brains sure taste a lot like Franco-American spaghetti."

"Did you have to put peanut butter inside the frogs' noses?"

It took a loud noise, a very loud noise, to be heard above all the chatter. The doorway of the haunted house banged open and a tall, white-sheeted ghost appeared.

"I," it rasped, breathing heavily, "am the ghost" — the voice echoed hollowly — "of Lighthouse Paaa-aark." The word became an eerie howl. "Where is my dawwwwwwg?"

CHAPTER
6

The racket in the wreck room stopped as though somebody had turned an Off switch. At the same moment, the lights dimmed. Only a shaded light at the foot of the stairs lit the room. In the silence, everyone turned to stare at the ghost.

It stood there, wavering from side to side, its white sheet fluttering. An eerie glow came from under the sheet. It was taller than a man, and maybe it had arms, because the sheet moved as though an arm moved beneath it. But where was its head? Did it *have* a head?

The top part of the sheet ended in a point.

"I came," it said in a hollow-sounding voice, "seeking my faithful dog." The word ended in a wail. "Whoooo-ooo has seen the hound of Lighthouse Park? Whoo-oo?"

Everyone moved closer together, clutching each other.

"I am your friend," moaned the ghost.

Nobody seemed to believe that. The space aliens huddled together. The clown and the ballerina backed away toward a wall.

"Who *is* that?" whispered Peanut.

"I don't know," muttered Jilly.

"I am your friend," the ghost repeated. "I must find the hound in order to save your lives. Can nobody tell me where the hound is?"

Nervous giggles broke the silence.

Peanut knew there were no such things as ghosts. But still — this one was spooky. She inched closer to Jilly. "If you planned this and didn't tell me, I'll be mad," she whispered.

"Didn't!" protested Jilly.

"Promise?"

51

"Promise."

"Weird!"

"Scary!"

The ghost let out a shuddering moan. "Let me tell you about my faithful lost hound. Once, long ago-ooo, in time before telling, I lived in a log cabin on the shore of the lake."

The ghost paused, breathing in hollowly, breathing out harshly, swaying from side to side. "With me were my beautiful wife, my strong young son, and my pretty little daughter. Protecting us all from the frightful creatures that roamed through the ancient forest was my faithful dog."

The hobos clustered together. Even the karate fighters seemed to be standing closer to each other.

The ghost continued. "We lived happily in our small cabin. The lake gave us fish to eat. The forest gave us rabbits. The apple tree outside our door gave us apples."

"Hey!" someone muttered. "There is an old apple tree in the park."

"Silence!" came the hoarse command. "Si-

52

lence, or I will let the hound enter here to tear you all limb from limb.

"Each day my faithful hound and I hunted and fished. My brave young son stayed at home to protect his dear mother and pretty little sister. In the evening, my hound and I brought home food, and my beautiful wife cooked it. After we ate, we sat before the fire and told tales of the long-ago times. The forest surrounding our cabin was black and filled with terrifying beings that howled in the blackness. But we were safe in our snug cabin."

The ghost moved. The sheet swayed.

"Look how it's lighted up from inside," whispered Jilly.

"The way it breathes — I've never heard anything breathe like that," said Peanut.

"It's like it's talking through a tin can or something," said Jilly.

"Silence!"

Nobody spoke. The room was filled with the ghost's hoarse breathing. Then it continued speaking. "We were safe, until one day at just this time of year. . . .

53

"I went out as usual that morning, my faithful hound at my heels, to hunt for our dinner. That evening, as I neared home, just before I stepped out from among the trees, I saw the outlines of a giant ship. A carved dragon rose from its prow and many oars lined its sides. Raiders! Raiders from some far land had come to my peaceful shore. I had heard of these raiders. They were giants who wore helmets of iron and carried swords the size of young trees. My beautiful wife! My pretty little daughter! My brave young son! Where were they? I leaped into the clearing.

"My cabin was in smoking ruins.

"My dear wife was" — the ghost's voice dropped to speak a single, horrifying word — "dead.

"My dear little daughter was — dead.

"My stalwart young son was — dead.

"I fought heroically. But soon I, too, was — dead.

"My faithful hound leaped at the foul murderers. With one stroke of an enormous sword, he was slain. Dead!

"Then, laughing — ha-ha-ha — the raiders returned to their ship and rowed away. Their evil laughter floated across the water. Ha-ha-ha.

"On that day, I became the ghost you see before you. I seek the ghost of my faithful hound, maddened with sorrow. He prowls the shore of a lake. Each year on this very night — when the moon is full — he kills someone, anyone, to avenge the foul slaying of my beautiful wife, my pretty little daughter, my stalwart young son — and me."

The ghost seemed to raise an arm — the sheet moved in the eerie light, swaying. "Have you seen my faithful hound? Tell me. So that I may save your young lives."

Nobody moved.

"Roverr-rr," wailed the ghost, "where are you—ou-ou. . . . "

"AAAAA-OOOOO!" came a howl from outside. "AAAAA-OOOOO!"

CHAPTER
7

Screaming erupted on all sides.

"That's the ghost hound," somebody wailed. "It's outside."

"Go look," yelled someone else.

"No!" another voice shrieked. "Don't look! It'll get you!"

In the noise and confusion, nobody saw a second ghost descending the basement stairs, carrying a small bundle of fluff. It added its own yelp to the commotion.

"AAAAA-OOOOO!" Another unearthly howl split the air.

"Baby!" yelled one of the hobos, making a dash for the door to the haunted house and the exit beyond.

The other hobos followed, bumping into the ballerina and the clown, pushing to get past them.

Peanut and Jilly got the connection at exactly the same moment.

"Baby!"

"Jennifer!"

"Dawn and Cheryl!"

Peanut and Jilly sprinted after the hobos, pushing through the sheets and curtains in the haunted house, emerging on the far side near the door to the yard.

The last of the hobos was just crawling out of the hairy tunnel. But the first one was already stepping through the door and into the yard.

A big sheepdog, all wagging tail, joyful woofs, and happy leaps, sent the hobo sprawl-

ing. Off came the hobo hat and out tumbled a blonde ponytail.

"Jennifer Patimkin!" gasped Jilly. "It *is* you!"

"What are you doing here?" exclaimed Peanut.

"Baby! How did you get out of the house?" Jennifer sat up, pulling off her mask and hugging the big dog. "There, lovey!" she cooed. "It's all right. No awful ghost dog is going to hurt you. I won't let it."

"Lovey!" Peanut looked as though she were gagging — which, with her green face, was very interesting.

The other hobos — Cheryl and Dawn, of course — clustered around Jennifer and Baby.

Kids poured out of the haunted house, pulling off their masks so they could see and talking excitedly.

"It wasn't the ghost dog howling." Space alien Erin looked relieved. "It was only Jennifer's dog."

"Hey! What's she doing here?" demanded abominable snowman Elvis.

"I thought the kids in Mr. Moore's class weren't invited," said ballerina Elena.

"Talk about nerve!" sniffed clown Courtney.

"What Dumbos, to think they could get away with this," said karate fighter Ollie.

"Her own dog gave her away," said Sherlock Holmes David.

Jennifer had scrambled to her feet. She looked boldly from Jilly to Peanut. "Ha-ha," she said. "Fooled you."

"Only for a while," Jilly said icily. "We'd have caught you. Honestly, your dog has better manners than you do. Baby knew you weren't supposed to be here. That's why she came and got you."

"You knew there wasn't room for all the classes," Peanut said hotly. "You knew the haunted house was only for us kids in Miss Kraft's class."

"Oh, what's two or three more people!" Jennifer said airily, laughing, showing toothy gaps where her teeth were blacked out.

"I mean," said Dawn, "it wasn't like everybody was jammed together or anything."

Emmy came to stand beside Jilly. "I thought Mr. Moore's class was having its own party at Derek Benson's house."

One by one the kids lined up behind Peanut and Jilly, staring at the hobos, speaking their minds.

"What you did isn't fair," said David.

"Didn't you know we'd catch you?" asked Elena.

"Didn't you wonder what we'd do when we caught you?" asked Ollie.

As they spoke, they all moved forward.

Jennifer stepped back. She laughed, but it wasn't a something's-funny laugh. It sounded like pretend-brave laughter. "Why, I just thought it would be a good joke."

"The joke's on you guys," added Cheryl, laughing slyly.

"Eyeball salad!" exclaimed Dawn. "Really! How childish!"

Nobody noticed Mr. Matthews and Grandpa Wayne step out into the yard.

"What's going on here?" Mr. Matthews asked in his easygoing way.

The three hobos turned and ran off into the darkness, with Baby bounding after them.

Her hands on her hips, her face crimson around all its witchy wrinkles, Jilly stared after them. "That Jennifer is a real . . . a real . . . glurk!" she sputtered.

"So are Dawn and Cheryl," said Peanut. "They should have their noses examined — because Jennifer leads them around by them. Their noses have to be getting longer."

"Want me to go get 'em?" asked Ollie, taking a karate pose, his hands raised.

Karate fighter Nate leaped forward to stand beside him. "These hands are trained to kill."

"All right now," said Mr. Matthews. "Save the mayhem for another time. What was that all about?"

"Party crashers!"

"Kids from Mr. Moore's class."

The voices tumbled over each other as everybody spoke at the same time.

"Jennifer's dog got out of their house and trailed her here."

"That's who was howling out here in the yard!"

"It wasn't the ghost hound of Lighthouse Park . . . seeking . . . revenge. . . . " The voice drifted into nothingness.

Silence descended on the darkened yard as everyone remembered what they had been doing when the eerie howl came from outdoors.

Then, "Where did the ghost who told the story go?" somebody asked.

"What ghost?" asked Mr. Matthews. He turned to Grandpa Wayne. "Did you see any ghosts in the basement just now?"

"Not when I walked through there a minute ago," said Grandpa. "Of course, I didn't exactly look around in all the corners."

Everyone dashed for the door. They made a shambles of the haunted house, pushing aside the sheets and curtains. Nobody paid any attention to the cobwebs or the tarantulas or the limp, sloshy rubber glove dangling from the ceiling. They crowded into the wreck room.

The lights were bright and the table was covered with a party cloth. Candles burned in glass hurricane shades and there were plastic flowers braided into a chain around the edge of the table. The delicious smell of hot chocolate rose from several pitchers. Mrs. Matthews and Mrs. Butterman were coming downstairs, carrying trays of taffy apples and haunted house gingerbread squares.

"Is anybody hungry?" asked Mrs. Matthews.

A wriggling bundle of fur bounced across the room and jumped at Peanut.

"Nibbsie!" said Peanut. "I thought we left you at home because of the cats. Who brought him?" she asked her mother.

"Oh, I guess Grandpa thought this was a party he shouldn't miss," said Mrs. Butterman. "Hang on to him. We'll take him home when we leave."

Everyone lost interest in hunting for the ghost. But they still chattered about him while they ate. Nobody would believe that Jilly didn't know who the ghost was.

64

"Honest," she said. "I don't know any more than you guys do."

"Could've been your brother," said David.

Jilly shook her head hard. "Couldn't be. The ghost was too tall to be Jerry."

"But how could you tell? I mean, his head ended in a point," David insisted.

"Your father?" asked Courtney.

"But it didn't sound like him," insisted Jilly, licking purple frosting off her fingers. "I mean, with all that weird breathing and that echoey voice. Maybe it was your grandpa," she said, turning to Peanut.

"It didn't sound like him, either," said Peanut. "But who else was here? I mean, what other man?"

Their glances locked.

"Mr. X!"

"I bet Miss Kraft put him up to it."

They raced upstairs and into the kitchen.

Mrs. Matthews and Grandma Wayne and Mrs. Butterman looked up from their coffee. "Did we forget something?" asked Mrs. Matthews.

"Miss Kraft!" gasped Jilly. "Where is she?"

"Oh, she and her friend went out to dinner," said Mrs. Butterman. "They were going to that new Mexican place on Dempster Street," she added, to Mrs. Butterman.

Disappointed, Jilly turned away.

But Peanut thought of something else. "When did they go?"

"Oh, ages ago," said Mrs. Matthews. "Right after she inspected all of your costumes."

"Ohhhhh."

So that was that. The ghost was not Mr. X.

Peanut and Jilly went back downstairs, just in time to see Ollie and Nate hauling a couple of big shopping bags in from outdoors.

"Happy un-birthday!" everybody yelled.

It was Jilly's turn to be surprised that evening. Her cheeks showed pink all around her witchy wrinkles. She felt suddenly shy and happy. The shopping bags were full of packages everyone had left outside when they came into the haunted house.

Pleased at the success of her plan, Peanut

stood watching, grinning as Jilly opened her un-presents.

There was a blue ballpoint pen on a cord to hang around her neck, and two glow-in-the-dark dinosaurs — an apatosaurus and a stegosaurus. There was pink cat stationery — that was from Peanut — and bubble bath and butterfly clips for her hair, and lots more. The most surprising un-present was a whole pound of Gummi Worms.

"Those are from me," Ollie said proudly. "I got the last ones they had at the Jewel. Hey," he added, remembering, "I thought there was going to be a prize for the best costume. So when are you going to give me my prize?"

"We were supposed to keep our masks on until the prize," said Emmy. "Only now we all know who everybody is."

"It's got to be fair," said David.

They decided to clap for the best costume.

Jilly held her witch hat over each person. Of course, each kid clapped hardest for himself. But the loudest clapping — and it came from

everybody — was for abominable snowman Elvis.

He won the prize, hands down. It was a back-scratcher. He hopped around, his big hairy feet flopping, scratching under his arms and down his back, giggling. And for once, nobody told him to stop.

CHAPTER 8

"I sure would like another Gummi Worm."

"But you'd have to brush your teeth again."

"Guess I won't."

"Gummi Worms! Only Ollie would think of that for a present."

"But it was an *un*-present."

Peanut and Jilly laughed softly. They were cozy in their pajamas, curled up on the beds in Jilly's room.

"You're still kind of an interesting pale green," said Jilly, studying Peanut's face.

"I wonder if black comes off teeth," Peanut said thoughtfully.

Jilly's eyes danced. "Maybe old Jennifer will have gray teeth for a while."

"And she won't be able to smile at the boys she likes," said Peanut.

"Wouldn't that be — *childish!*" said Peanut.

They giggled until their beds shook.

"Do you suppose we'll ever find out who the ghost was?" Peanut asked when she finally stopped laughing.

"It just had to be my dad," said Jilly. "But he only laughed when I asked him. He'll never tell."

"I wonder how the ghost story was going to end," said Peanut. "I mean, what would have happened if Baby hadn't come to the door and howled?"

There was a sound at the door. It opened a crack. "Can I come in there?" asked Jackie.

"Sure. Come on, Jack-O," called Jilly.

"Well, first you've got to turn off the light," said Jackie.

"Why?" asked Jilly.

"Because I'm going to scare you," said Jackie.

Peanut snapped off the bedside lamp. "It's off," she called.

The door opened wide and Jackie leaped into the room holding a flashlight under his chin. His face looked weird, with parts of it in dark shadow and parts of it harshly lit. "I'm a monster," he announced.

71

"Boy, you really scared me," said Jilly. "Hey — I thought you lost your flashlight."

"Daddy had it," said Jackie. "He gave it back to me just now so I could keep it next to me tonight in case it gets too dark in my room."

Mrs. Matthews appeared behind him. "Come along, Jackie. It's time to unwind and go to sleep. I'll read you a story."

"A monster story?" asked Jackie.

"How about Peter Rabbit?" said Mrs. Matthews, taking his hand. "Don't talk too long, girls," she added, closing the door.

"The flashlight!" said Jilly.

"The ghost was lit up from inside the sheet," said Peanut.

"Then it *was* my dad," said Jilly.

They didn't turn the lamp back on. The room was silent.

After a while Peanut spoke into the darkness. "It takes hours and hours to make eyeball salad. I thought I'd never finish peeling grapes."

"Did you see Ollie's face when he ate some?" said Jilly. "He acts like he isn't scared of

72

anything and then he has to do whatever he says."

Peanut punched her pillow and bunched it up under her cheek. "He sort of walks into his own traps."

Again the room was still.

Jilly spoke around a yawn. "Making the tape recording was fun, too. There sure are a lot of different ways to scream and moan."

A minute passed before Peanut answered. Her voice seemed to come from a long way off. "The kids sure did screech a lot."

"It was," breathed Jilly, "the neatest . . . haunted . . . house."

"Best one," murmured Peanut, "I ever . . . visited . . . in . . . my. . . . "

The moon shone in at the windows. It was a full moon. And not a single dog anywhere nearby howled at it.